CORDUROY'S Hike

A Viking Easy-to-Read

Story by **Alison Inches**

Illustrations by **Allan Eitzen**

Based on the characters created by
Don Freeman

VIKING

VIKING
Published by the Penguin Group
Penguin Putnam Books for Young Readers,
345 Hudson Street, New York, New York 10014, U.S.A.
Penguin Books Ltd, 27 Wrights Lane, London W8 5TZ, England
Penguin Books Australia Ltd, Ringwood, Victoria, Australia
Penguin Books Canada Ltd, 10 Alcorn Avenue, Toronto, Ontario, Canada M4V 3B2
Penguin Books (N.Z.) Ltd, 182-190 Wairau Road, Auckland 10, New Zealand

Penguin Books Ltd, Registered Offices: Harmondsworth, Middlesex, England

First published in 2001 by Viking,
a division of Penguin Putnam Books for Young Readers.

1 3 5 7 9 10 8 6 4 2

Copyright © Penguin Putnam Inc., 2001
Text by Alison Inches
Illustrations by Allan Eitzen
All rights reserved

LIBRARY OF CONGRESS CATALOGING-IN-PUBLICATION DATA
Inches, Alison.
Corduroy's hike / by Alison Inches ; illustrated by Allan Eitzen ;
based on the character created by Don Freeman.
p. cm. — (Viking easy-to-read)
Summary: Corduroy sneaks into Lisa's backpack when she goes on a hiking
trip and has quite an adventure when he gets lost along the trail.
ISBN 0-670-88945-8 (hardcover)
[1. Teddy bears—Fiction. 2. Toys—Fiction. 3. Hiking—Fiction.] I.
Eitzen, Allan, ill. II. Freeman, Don. III. Title. IV. Series.
PZ7.I355 Co 2001
[E]—dc21
2001000509

Viking ® and Easy-to-Read ® are registered trademarks of Penguin Putnam Inc.

Printed in Singapore
Set in Bookman

Reading Level 1.8

CORDUROY'S Hike

Lisa checked her backpack.

Peanut butter sandwich.

Juice.

Hat.

Jacket.

"You have to stay here, Corduroy," Lisa said.

"You might get lost on a hike."

Lisa began to brush her hair.

I will not get lost, thought Corduroy.

He crawled into the backpack.

I will be safe in here.

Beep! Beep! The bus had come.

Lisa sat next to Susan.

"What did you bring?" asked Susan.

Lisa opened her backpack.

"A peanut butter sandwich.

Juice.

And *Corduroy!*

How did you get in here?

You might get lost on a hike."

"Corduroy will be fine," said Susan.

"He will be safe in your backpack."

Lisa hoped Susan was right.

At the park,

Lisa and Susan found a stream

with a bridge over it.

They dropped sticks into the water.

Then they ran across the bridge.

The sticks came out the other side.

"I see mine!" they cried.

Then it was time to hike.

Lisa put on her hat

and her backpack.

Off they went.

Bounce! Bounce! Bounce!

Corduroy bounced along in the backpack.

The class hiked higher and higher.

"I can see a farm!" said Susan.

"I can see a church!" said Lisa.

I can't see a thing, thought Corduroy.

Corduroy poked his head out.

That's better, thought Corduroy.

Now I can see, too.

Bounce! Bounce! Bounce!

Corduroy bounced along in the backpack.

This is fun, thought Corduroy.

Look, no hands!

Whoops!

Corduroy bounced out of the backpack . . .

Thud!

. . . and onto the trail.

He rolled over and over

and stopped facedown in the dust.

Lisa will pick me up, thought Corduroy.

But Lisa did not pick him up.

Lisa will come back for me.

But Lisa did not come back for Corduroy.

Oh dear, thought Corduroy.

I think I am lost.

Soon two hikers came by.

They picked up Corduroy.

"You must have an owner," said one hiker.

She set Corduroy on a branch.

"Your owner will see you up here," she said.

Corduroy waited for Lisa.

He sang songs.

He watched the birds.

Then he saw a Cub Scout troop

hiking up the trail.

"Look!" said a Cub Scout. "A bear!"

The Cub Scout picked up Corduroy

and tossed him in the air.

Then he tossed him to another boy.

They tossed Corduroy back and forth.

Corduroy felt like a football.

Another boy ran ahead.

Corduroy flew through the air.

They did it again.

And again.

And again.

Then, **thud!**

Corduroy landed on the side of the trail.

The Cub Scouts walked on.

Corduroy tried to stand up.

He felt dizzy.

He tipped to one side.

He tipped to the other.

Then Corduroy tipped over.

Splash!

He fell into the stream.

Oh my! thought Corduroy.

The water took Corduroy away.

It took him over rocks

and under a bridge . . .

Then, **zoom!**

Corduroy zoomed over a waterfall.

He zoomed under another bridge
and, **bonk!** stopped on a rock.
Oh, dear, thought Corduroy.
I think I am stuck.
And I am cold.
And wet.
And more lost.

Soon it began to get dark.

The class came back down the trail

and into the parking lot.

Lisa sat down

and stared at her feet.

Corduroy was gone.

He had been missing since lunch.

She had looked everywhere for him.

The teacher clapped her hands.

"Time to get on the bus!"

Lisa sat next to the window.

Susan sat beside her.

"We were playing the stick

game again," she said.

Lisa nodded her head.

"My sticks all came out on the other side."

Lisa nodded again.

"Something else came out

on the other side, too," said Susan.

Susan handed Corduroy to Lisa.

"Corduroy!" cried Lisa.

She hugged her wet bear.

"I'm so glad I've got you."

Corduroy thought, *I'm so glad*

you've got me, too.